THE GRAPHIC NOVEL
Charles Dickens

Adapted from an original script by Sean Michael Wilson

Australia • Brazil • Canada • Mexico • Singapore • United Kingdom • United States

Cengage

A Christmas Carol: The Graphic Novel
Charles Dickens

Script by Sean Michael Wilson

Publisher: Sherrise Roehr

Editor in Chief: Clive Bryant

Managing Development Editor:
John Hicks

Associate Development Editor:
Cécile Engeln

Director of U.S. Marketing:
Jim McDonough

Assistant Marketing Manager: Jide Iruka

Director of Content Production:
Michael Burggren

Associate Content Project Manager:
Mark Rzeszutek

Print Buyer: Susan Spencer

Design and Layout: Jo Wheeler and
Jenny Placentino

Pencils: Mike Collins

Inks: David Roach

Coloring: James Offredi

Lettering: Terry Wiley

Compositor: MPS Limited, A Macmillan
Company

For product information and technology assistance, contact us at **Cengage Customer & Sales Support, 1-800-354-9706 or support.cengage.com.**

For permission to use material from this text or product, submit all requests online at **www.copyright.com**.

ISBN: 978-1-4240-4287-6

Cengage
200 Pier 4 Boulevard
Boston, MA 02210
USA

Cengage is a leading provider of customized learning solutions with employees residing in nearly 40 different countries and sales in more than 125 countries around the world. Find your local representative at:
www.cengage.com.

To learn more about Cengage platforms and services, register or access your online learning solution, or purchase materials for your course, visit **www.cengage.com.**

Printed in the United States of America
Print Number: 11   Print Year: 2023

Contents

A Christmas Carol

Characters

Ghost of Jacob Marley

Ghost of Christmas Past

Ebenezer Scrooge

Ghost of Christmas Present

Ghost of Christmas to Come

Bob Cratchit
Scrooge's clerk

Mrs. Cratchit
Bob's wife

Martha Cratchit
Bob's oldest daughter

Peter Cratchit
Bob's oldest son

Belinda Cratchit
Bob's second daughter

Cratchit children

Tiny Tim Cratchit
Bob's youngest son

Fan
Scrooge's sister

School principal

Characters

Mr. and Mrs. Fezziwig

Dick Wilkins
Scrooge's fellow apprentice

Belle
As a girl

Belle
As a married woman

Belle's husband

Fred
Scrooge's nephew

Alice
Fred's wife

Alice's sister

Topper
Fred's Friend

Ignorance and Want

Old Joe
Shop owner

Cleaning woman

Mrs. Dilber
Washerwoman

Undertaker

Caroline and her husband

A Christmas Carol

Today, Christmas is a big, important holiday. People decorate Christmas trees, sing Christmas carols, send Christmas cards, and buy Christmas presents. Most people don't work on Christmas. They spend time with their families. But Christmas was not always like this. When Charles Dickens published *A Christmas Carol* **back** in 1843, Christmas was only becoming a big, important holiday.

In Victorian England, middle-class families could afford big Christmas celebrations for the first time. People took the day off from work and enjoyed a large meal with their families. Mass-produced goods — toys and other items — were cheaper than ever before. Middle-class families could now afford presents for their loved ones.

But poor families could not celebrate Christmas like middle-class families. Christmas was too expensive for them. And they usually had to work. Every day — including Christmas — was a struggle.

Imagine a man who had money but did not want to share it. Imagine a man who knew about the struggles of poor families but did not want to help them. Imagine a cold, selfish man … do you think he could change?

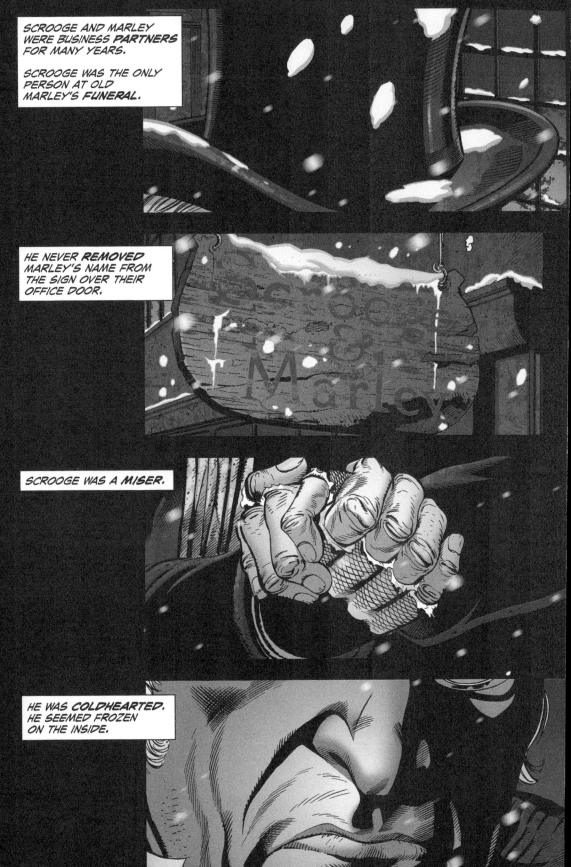

SCROOGE AND MARLEY WERE BUSINESS **PARTNERS** FOR MANY YEARS.

SCROOGE WAS THE ONLY PERSON AT OLD MARLEY'S **FUNERAL.**

HE NEVER **REMOVED** MARLEY'S NAME FROM THE SIGN OVER THEIR OFFICE DOOR.

SCROOGE WAS A **MISER.**

HE WAS **COLDHEARTED.** HE SEEMED FROZEN ON THE INSIDE.

HEAT COULDN'T WARM HIM, AND COLD COULDN'T *CHILL* HIM.

NOBODY EVER STOPPED SCROOGE ON THE STREET TO TALK TO HIM.

EVEN *BLIND* MEN'S DOGS *GUIDED* THEIR OWNERS AWAY FROM SCROOGE!

BUT SCROOGE DIDN'T CARE. ACTUALLY, HE LIKED IT THAT WAY.

SCROOGE LIKED TO **KEEP AN EYE ON** HIS **CLERK.**

SCROOGE ONLY **ALLOWED** HIS **CLERK** TO HAVE A TINY FIRE TO WARM HIMSELF.

HE WAS VERY COLD. HE WARMED HIMSELF WITH HIS CANDLE.

WE ARE SURE YOU ARE AS **GENEROUS** AS HE WAS.

THAT WAS TRUE. THEY WERE BOTH **MISERS**!

AT THIS TIME OF YEAR, MR. SCROOGE, WE SHOULD REMEMBER POOR PEOPLE AND GIVE TO **CHARITY**.

SO MANY PEOPLE DON'T EVEN HAVE **BASIC NECESSITIES**.

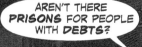

AREN'T THERE **PRISONS** FOR PEOPLE WITH **DEBTS**?

THERE ARE PLENTY OF **PRISONS**.

AND **WORKHOUSES** FOR POOR PEOPLE?

UNFORTUNATELY, YES.

DO WE STILL HAVE THE **POOR LAW**?

YES, SIR.

OH! I WAS AFRAID THAT **PARLIAMENT** HAD DONE AWAY WITH IT.

17

THERE ISN'T ENOUGH ROOM FOR ALL THE POOR PEOPLE. AND MANY PEOPLE WOULD RATHER DIE THAN GO THERE.

IF THEY WOULD RATHER DIE, THEN THEY SHOULD HURRY UP AND DO IT.

GOOD AFTERNOON, GENTLEMEN!

SCROOGE CONTINUED WORKING. HE THOUGHT HE HAD HANDLED THE CONVERSATION WELL.

AS THE DAY PASSED, IT GOT EVEN COLDER.

GOD REST YOU **MERRY** GENTLEMEN! LET NOTHING YOU **DISMAY!**

IT WAS TIME TO CLOSE THE **COUNTINGHOUSE** FOR THE EVENING.

YOU WANT TO TAKE TOMORROW OFF, I SUPPOSE?

IF THAT'S OK, SIR.

IT ISN'T. AND IT'S NOT FAIR.

YOU WOULD THINK IT WAS WRONG IF I PAID YOU LESS.

BUT YOU THINK I SHOULD PAY YOU FOR A DAY YOU DON'T WORK.

SCROOGE ATE HIS LONELY DINNER AT THE USUAL PLACE ...

... AND WENT HOME TO BED.

HE LIVED ALONE IN OLD MARLEY'S HOUSE.

FOR A LONG TIME, SCROOGE HADN'T THOUGHT ABOUT MARLEY – UNTIL THOSE MEN MENTIONED HIS NAME.

AS HE CLIMBED THE STAIRS ...

IT WAS VERY DARK.

BUT DARKNESS DIDN'T COST ANYTHING, SO SCROOGE LIKED IT.

HE CHECKED ALL THE ROOMS. NOTHING WAS OUT OF PLACE.

... SCROOGE THOUGHT HE SAW A *HEARSE*.

HAPPY THAT EVERYTHING WAS AS IT SHOULD BE, SCROOGE LOCKED THE DOOR.

25

BAH HUMBUG!

HE SAW AN OLD **BELL** THAT MARLEY HAD USED TO CALL **SERVANTS.**

GDANG GDANG GDANG

THEN,
SILENCE ...

OOOOHHHHH! AAARGHHH!
OOAARGH! AAAAH!
CLANK
CLANK
CHINK CHINK
RATTLE
RATTLE

HAVE MERCY!

DO YOU BELIEVE IN ME NOW?

I DO! BUT WHY ARE YOU HERE?

EVERYONE SHOULD TRAVEL AND ENJOY LIFE WHILE THEY ARE ALIVE. OTHERWISE, WE HAVE TO TRAVEL AFTER WE DIE –

– WANDERING THE WORLD AND WATCHING HAPPY PEOPLE.

OOOHHHHH AAAAHHH!

AAHHH!!

CLANK CLANK

RATTLE

33

JACOB, SAY SOMETHING TO CHEER ME UP!

I CAN'T.

I CAN'T REST, I CAN'T STAY ANYWHERE.

I NEVER WALKED BEYOND OUR OFFICES WHEN I WAS ALIVE.

NOW THERE ARE MANY LONG JOURNEYS AHEAD OF ME!

YOU MUST BE A SLOW TRAVELER! IT'S BEEN SEVEN YEARS, JACOB!

SLOW!!

NO REST! NO PEACE!

CLANK

CLANK

THE PAIN OF REGRET!

CLANK

I SUFFER THE MOST AT CHRISTMAS.

OH, WHY DIDN'T I LOVE CHRISTMAS MORE?

I HAVE TO LEAVE SOON.

I SAT BESIDE YOU FOR MANY DAYS. YOU COULDN'T SEE ME.

TONIGHT, I'M HERE TO BRING YOU A MESSAGE. YOU STILL HAVE A CHANCE TO AVOID THE SUFFERING THAT I'M EXPERIENCING.

THANK YOU!

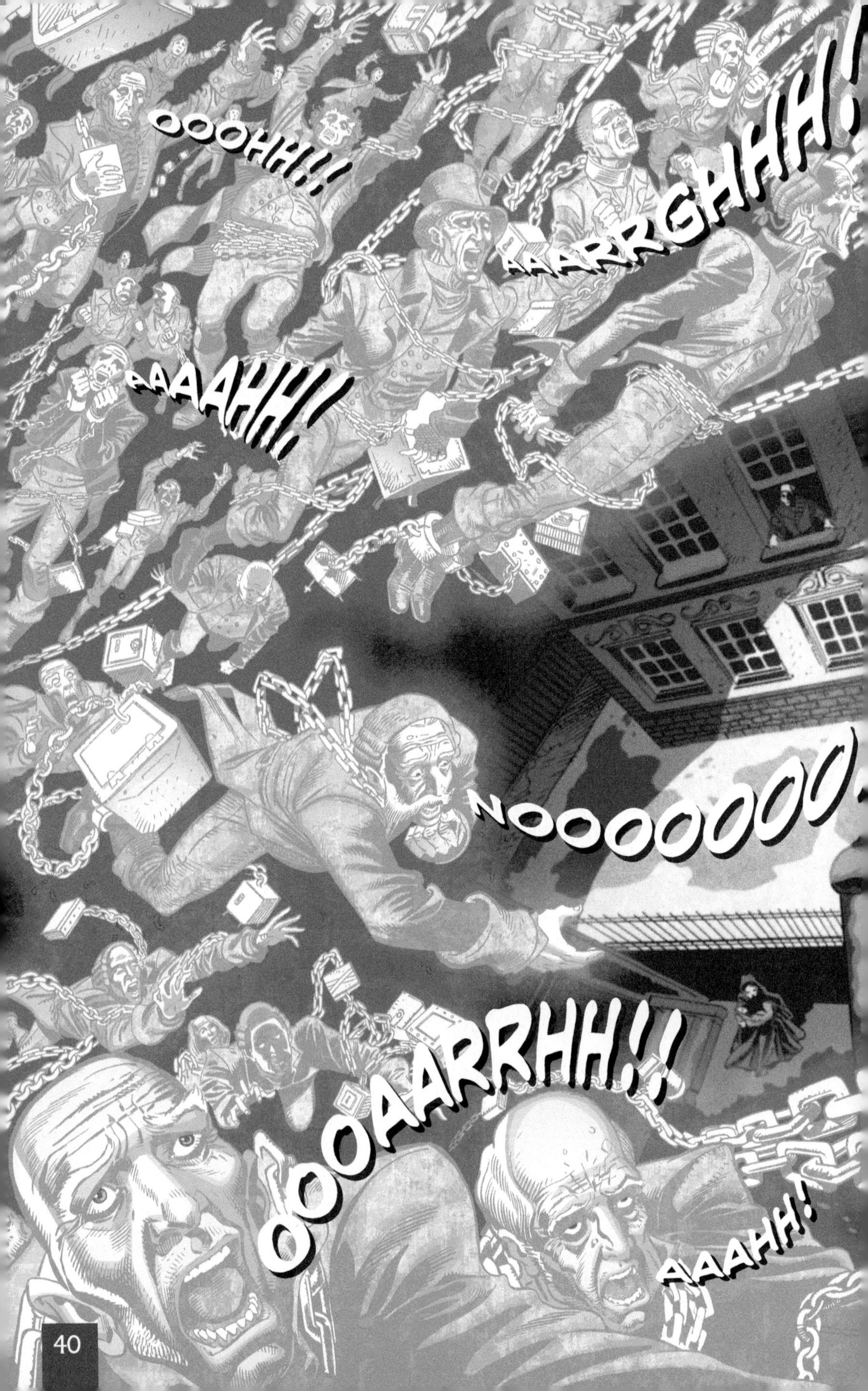
OOOHH!!
AAARRGHHH!
AAAAHH!
NOOOOOOOO!
OOOAARRHH!!
AAAHH!

DONG!
DONG!
DONG!
DONG!
DONG!
DONG!
DONG!
DONG!
DONG!
DONG!
DONG!
DONG!...
TWELVE? BUT I WENT TO BED SOME TIME AFTER TWO O'CLOCK. THE CLOCK MUST BE WRONG.

DING DONG!
TWELVE FIFTEEN.
DING DONG!
TWELVE THIRTY.
DING DONG!
TWELVE FORTY-FIVE.
DING DONG!
ONE O'CLOCK!
DONG!

47

SCROOGE CRIED
WHEN HE SAW HIS
YOUNG, POOR,
FORGOTTEN SELF.

I WISH ...

What's the matter?

OH, NOTHING.

THERE WAS A BOY SINGING A CHRISTMAS *CAROL* OUTSIDE MY HOUSE LAST NIGHT.

I SHOULD HAVE GIVEN HIM SOMETHING.

Let's see another Christmas!

MY DEAR BROTHER!

I CAME TO BRING YOU HOME!

HOME?

YES!

HOME. FOR EVER AND EVER.

FATHER IS SO MUCH NICER THAN HE USED TO BE.

I ASKED HIM IF YOU COULD COME HOME, AND HE SAID YES!

AND YOU'RE NEVER COMING BACK HERE AGAIN!

THIS YEAR, WE'LL HAVE THE HAPPIEST CHRISTMAS IN THE WHOLE WORLD!

YOU ARE QUITE A SISTER!

THE SCHOOL PRINCIPAL APPEARED.

BRING **MASTER** SCROOGE'S TRUNK!

THE PRINCIPAL TOOK SCROOGE AND HIS SISTER TO THE **PARLOR.** THE DRIVER PUT SCROOGES'S TRUNK INTO THE **CARRIAGE.**

GOOD-BYE, SIR.

IT'S JUST ... I WISH I COULD SPEAK TO MY **CLERK** NOW.

I have to leave soon. Hurry!

SCROOGE SAW HIMSELF AGAIN. HE WAS OLDER THIS TIME.

I DON'T MATTER TO YOU.

HA HA!

YAY!!

DADDY!!

I SAW AN OLD FRIEND OF YOURS TODAY.

WHO WAS IT?

GUESS!

HA, HA! I DON'T KNOW ...

... MR. SCROOGE?

YES. MR. SCROOGE! HE WAS SITTING ALONE IN HIS OFFICE –

– WHILE HIS PARTNER IS LYING ON HIS DEATHBED!

SNOOOORE...

SNOOOR-UH!

DONG!

IT WAS ONE O'CLOCK AGAIN.

SCROOGE WOKE UP JUST IN TIME TO MEET THE SECOND *GHOST.*

FIVE MINUTES ...

TEN MINUTES ...

FIFTEEN MINUTES PASSED.

BUT NO ONE CAME.

?!?

SCROOGE, COME IN!

WHERE'S MARTHA?

SHE ISN'T COMING.

SHE ISN'T COMING? ON CHRISTMAS DAY?

!!!

HOW'S TINY TIM?

HE'S WONDERFUL. SOMETIMES HE GETS LONELY AND SAYS THE STRANGEST THINGS.

HE SAID THAT HE HOPED THE PEOPLE IN THE CHURCHYARD SAW HIM. BECAUSE HE CAN'T WALK, HE THOUGHT THEY MIGHT ENJOY REMEMBERING WHO HELPS **LAME** PEOPLE WALK AGAIN

AND **BLIND** PEOPLE SEE.

BOB'S VOICE *TREMBLED* AS HE SAID THIS ...

THERE WAS ENOUGH FOOD TO FEED THE WHOLE FAMILY.

THE DINNER PLATES WERE CLEARED. DESSERT PLATES WERE PUT ON THE TABLE. MRS. CRATCHIT LEFT THE ROOM.

OH! A DELICIOUS DESSERT!

EVERYONE HELPED CLEAN UP AFTER DINNER.

83

SCROOGE AND THE GHOST WALKED ALONG THE STREETS.

THE GHOST GAVE JOY TO EVERYONE THEY PASSED.

WHERE ARE WE?
THIS IS WHERE THE COAL MINERS LIVE.
THEY KNOW WHO I AM!
FIVE GOLD RINGS!!
... AND A PARTRIDGE IN A PEAR TREE.
THEY DIDN'T STAY LONG ...

MERRY CHRISTMAS!

MERRY CHRISTMAS!

SCROOGE AND THE **GHOST** CONTINUED ...

... OUT TO THE **SEA** ...

... WHERE THEY FOUND A SHIP.

♪ OH COME, ALL YE FAITHFUL, ♪ JOYFUL AND TRIUMPHANT ... ♪

TO HIS SURPRISE, SCROOGE HEARD A LOUD LAUGH.

HA, HA!
HA, HA, HA!

IT BELONGED TO HIS *NEPHEW*.

HE SAID THAT CHRISTMAS WAS *HUMBUG*!

THAT'S TERRIBLE, FRED!

HE'S A FUNNY OLD FELLOW.

HE *PUNISHES* HIMSELF. I HAVE NOTHING BAD TO SAY ABOUT HIM.

I'M SURE HE IS VERY RICH, FRED.

HIS MONEY DOESN'T DO HIM ANY GOOD.

HE DOESN'T DO ANY GOOD WITH HIS MONEY.

89

THEY *TRAVELED* FAR AND WIDE ...

... *SPREADING* HAPPINESS ALONG THE WAY.

IT SEEMED THAT THE ENTIRE CHRISTMAS SEASON WAS *SQUEEZED* INTO THIS VERY LONG NIGHT. THE *GHOST* LOOKED OLDER.

ARE *GHOSTS'* LIVES SHORT?

MY LIFE ON THIS EARTH IS VERY SHORT.

IT ENDS TONIGHT AT MIDNIGHT.

IT'S ALMOST TIME.

WHAT IS THAT?

IS IT A FOOT OR A *CLAW?*

LOOK !!

TIME IS PRECIOUS TO ME.
LET'S GO, GHOST!
NO. I DON'T KNOW MUCH ABOUT IT.
I JUST KNOW THAT HE'S DEAD.
WHEN DID HE DIE?
LAST NIGHT.

HOW ARE YOU?

HOW ARE YOU?

WELL! HE'S FINALLY **MET HIS MAKER!**

THAT'S WHAT I HEARD.

YOU, TOO!

COLD, ISN'T IT?

WELL, IT IS WINTER. HAVE A GOOD MORNING!

SCROOGE WAS SURPRISED THAT THEY WERE WATCHING SUCH *TRIVIAL* CONVERSATIONS.

SCROOGE LOOKED AROUND AND TRIED TO FIND HIMSELF, BUT HE DIDN'T SEE HIMSELF ANYWHERE.

THEY WENT TO A BAD PART OF TOWN.

EVERYTHING WAS DIRTY. IT WAS FULL OF CRIME AND SADNESS.

THERE WAS A SMALL, DIRTY SHOP THAT SOLD ALL KINDS OF OLD THINGS.

OLD JOE SAT SURROUNDED BY THE THINGS HE BOUGHT AND SOLD.

THE THREE OF US ARE HERE TOGETHER, EH, OLD JOE!

THIS IS THE PERFECT PLACE!

COME INSIDE. I'M GOING TO CLOSE THE DOOR.

SCREEEECH!!

COME IN!
EVERYONE HAS A RIGHT TO **TAKE CARE OF** THEMSELVES – HE ALWAYS DID.
TRUE.
COME ON, DON'T BE AFRAID. HE WON'T MISS THESE THINGS.
HE'S DEAD.

OLD JOE WROTE HOW MUCH EACH ITEM WAS WORTH ON THE WALL.

YOUR STUFF IS WORTH THIS MUCH.

WHO'S NEXT?

I ALWAYS GIVE LADIES TOO MUCH.

IT'S MY WEAKNESS. THAT'S HOW I RUIN MYSELF.

THAT'S HOW MUCH ALL YOUR STUFF IS WORTH. I WON'T GIVE YOU A PENNY MORE.

NOW, LOOK AT MY STUFF, JOE.
CURTAINS?
CURTAINS!
YOU TOOK THEM DOWN, RINGS AND ALL - WITH HIM LYING THERE?
I DID.
YOU'LL DO ANYTHING FOR MONEY!

NO! I CAN'T LOOK UNDER THERE!

PLEASE, SHOW ME SOMEONE WHO FEELS ANYTHING ABOUT THIS MAN'S DEATH.

THE *GHOST* *SPREAD* ITS *ROBE* OVER SCROOGE LIKE A WING ...

I WENT TO HIS HOUSE LAST NIGHT. I WAS GOING TO ASK HIM FOR MORE TIME.
A WOMAN TOLD ME THAT HE WAS DEAD.
HE WAS SO SICK! HE WAS DYING!
WHO DO WE PAY INSTEAD?

HE SAID TO LET HIM KNOW IF HE COULD DO ANYTHING FOR US.

IT WAS AS IF HE HAD KNOWN TINY TIM — AND FELT OUR SADNESS WITH US.

HE'S A GOOD MAN!

HE MIGHT EVEN GET PETER A GOOD JOB.

DID YOU HEAR THAT, PETER?

AND THEN PETER COULD GO INTO BUSINESS FOR HIMSELF.

I DOUBT IT!

EBENEZER SCROOGE
NO, GHOST!
OH, NO. NO!
GHOST! LISTEN TO ME!
I AM NOT THE MAN I USED TO BE.
I HAVE CHANGED.
WHY WOULD YOU SHOW THIS TO ME IF THERE WASN'T ANY HOPE?
THE GHOST'S HAND STARTED TO SHAKE.

GHOST, TELL ME THAT I CAN CHANGE MY FUTURE!
I WILL CELEBRATE CHRISTMAS.
I WILL LIVE IN THE PAST, THE PRESENT, AND THE FUTURE.
I WILL REMEMBER THE LESSONS I HAVE LEARNED.
OH, TELL ME THAT I CAN CHANGE WHAT THIS HEADSTONE SAYS!

HE WAS BACK IN HIS OWN ROOM.

BEST OF ALL, HE HAD HIS LIFE BACK. AND HE COULD LIVE HIS LIFE DIFFERENTLY!

I WILL LIVE IN THE PAST, THE PRESENT, AND THE FUTURE!

OH, JACOB MARLEY! **PRAISE** GOD AND CHRISTMASTIME FOR THIS!

MY CURTAINS ARE STILL HERE!

I CAN CHANGE MY FUTURE!

I DON'T EVEN KNOW WHAT DAY IT IS. I DON'T KNOW HOW LONG I WAS WITH THE **GHOSTS**.

DING DONG!
DING DONG!

HELLO THERE!

DING DING DONG! DING DING DONG! DING DONG! DING DONG! DONG!

DING DONG! DING DONG!

WHAT DAY IS IT TODAY?

DING DONG! DING DONG!

HUH?

DING DONG! DING DONG! DING DONG!

WHAT DAY IS IT TODAY, DEAR BOY?

IT'S CHRISTMAS DAY, SIR!

I'LL SEND IT TO BOB CRATCHIT. HE WON'T KNOW WHERE IT CAME FROM! IT'S BIGGER THAN TINY TIM!

HE WENT DOWNSTAIRS, OPENED THE DOOR, AND WAITED FOR THE TURKEY.

AS HE STOOD THERE, HE LOOKED AT HIS *DOOR KNOCKER*.

I WILL LOVE THIS WONDERFUL *DOOR KNOCKER* AS LONG AS I LIVE!

HERE'S THE TURKEY.

HELLO! **MERRY** CHRISTMAS!

IT'S TOO BIG TO CARRY ALL THE WAY TO BOB CRATCHIT'S HOME.

PLEASE TAKE A CAB.

HA, HA, HA!

HE CHUCKLED AS HE WALKED BACK INSIDE.

HE SAT DOWN AND LAUGHED UNTIL HE CRIED.

THEN HE DRESSED IN HIS BEST CLOTHES ...

... AND WENT OUT INTO THE STREETS.

GOOD MORNING, SIR! **MERRY** CHRISTMAS TO YOU!

MERRY CHRISTMAS TO YOU, TOO!

MY DEAR SIR, I HOPE YOU WERE SUCCESSFUL YESTERDAY.

MR. SCROOGE?

YES. I'M SORRY FOR THE WAY I TREATED YOU.

Please, will you ...

MY DEAR SIR, ARE YOU SERIOUS?

I AM. AND NOT A PENNY LESS!

I DON'T KNOW WHAT TO SAY

YOU DON'T HAVE TO SAY ANYTHING.

THANK YOU.

NOT AT ALL! THANK YOU. AND **BLESS** YOU!

HE WENT TO CHURCH ...

... AND WALKED WITH THE PEOPLE IN THE STREETS.

EVERYTHING HE SAW MADE HIM HAPPY.

IN THE AFTERNOON, HE VISITED HIS **NEPHEW'S** HOUSE.

IS YOUR **MASTER** HOME, MY DEAR?

YES, SIR.

WHERE IS HE?

HE'S IN THE DINING ROOM, SIR.

THANK YOU. HE KNOWS ME. I'LL JUST GO IN, MY DEAR.

I'LL PAY YOU MORE AND TRY TO HELP YOUR **STRUGGLING** FAMILY. WE CAN DISCUSS IT THIS AFTERNOON.

START THE FIRE AND GET MORE COAL, BOB!

SCROOGE DID EVEN MORE THAN HE SAID HE WOULD DO.

TINY TIM DID NOT DIE. SCROOGE WAS LIKE HIS SECOND FATHER.

SCROOGE BECAME A GOOD MAN.

SOME PEOPLE LAUGHED WHEN THEY SAW HOW HE HAD CHANGED. BUT SCROOGE DIDN'T CARE.

HE WAS HAPPY JUST TO SEE THEM LAUGHING.

HE WAS HAPPY IN HIS HEART. AND THAT WAS GOOD ENOUGH FOR HIM.

SCROOGE NEVER SAW ANOTHER *GHOST*. AND HE BECAME KNOWN FOR *OBSERVING* CHRISTMAS BETTER THAN ANYONE ELSE.

HOPEFULLY, WE CAN ALL BE KNOWN FOR THAT. AS TINY TIM SAID ...

GOD *BLESS* US, EVERY ONE!

A Christmas Carol

The End

Glossary

A

afford /əffɔrd/ – (affords, affording, afforded) If you cannot afford to do something or allow it to happen, you must not do it or must prevent it from happening because it would be harmful or embarrassing to you.

Ali Baba /ɒli bɒbʌ/ – Ali Baba is a woodcutter in the *Arabian Nights* stories who enters the cave of the Forty Thieves by using the password "open sesame."

allow /əlaʊ/ – (allows, allowing, allowed) If you are allowed something, you are given permission to have it or are given it.

anonymously /ənɒnɪməsli/ – If you do something anonymously, you do not let people know that you were the person who did it.

apply /əplaɪ/ – (applies, applying, applied) If something such as a rule or a remark applies to a person or a situation, it is relevant to them.

avoid /əvɔɪd/ – (avoids, avoiding, avoided) If you avoid something unpleasant that might happen, you take action in order to prevent it from happening.

B

basic necessities /beɪsɪk nɪsɛsɪtiz/ – Basic necessities are the simplest, least luxurious goods and services someone must have in order to live.

be left alone /bi lɛft əloʊn/ – If you want to be left alone, you want the people around you to go away and stop bothering you so you can be by yourself.

bell /bɛl/ – (bells) A bell is a device, usually a hollow object with a loose piece inside of it, that makes a ringing sound when its sides are struck and is used to attract people's attention.

blame /bleɪm/ – (blames, blaming, blamed) If you blame a person or thing for something bad, you believe or say that they are responsible for it or that they caused it.

bless /blɛs/ – (blesses, blessing, blessed) Bless is used in expressions like "God bless" or "bless you" to express affection, thanks, or good wishes.

blind /blaɪnd/ – The blind are people who are unable to see because their eyes are damaged.

blindfolded /blaɪndfoʊldɪd/ – If someone is blindfolded, that person has a strip of cloth tied over their eyes so they cannot see.

bound /baʊnd/ – If something or someone has been bound, that person or thing has had rope, string, tape, or some other material tied around them so that they are held firmly.

broke /broʊk/ – If you are broke, you have no money.

bury /bɛri/ – (buries, burying, buried) To bury something means to put it into a hole in the ground and cover it up. To bury a dead person means to put their body into a grave and cover it with earth.

C

cap /kæp/ – (caps) Something that serves as a cover or protection especially for a tip, knob, or end.

carol /kærəl/ – (carols) A carol is a Christian religious song that is sung at Christmas.

carriage /kærɪdʒ/ – (carriages) A carriage is an old-fashioned vehicle pulled by horses.

cast /kæst/ – (casts, casting) If something casts a light or shadow somewhere, it causes it to appear there.

celebrate /sɛlɪbreɪt/ – (celebrates, celebrating, celebrated) If you celebrate something, you do something enjoyable because of a special occasion.

charity /tʃærɪti/ – (charities) A charity is an organization which raises money in order to help people who are ill, disabled, or very poor. If you give money to charity, you give it to a charity.

cheer someone up /tʃɪər sʌmwʌn ʌp/ – (cheers someone up, cheering someone up, cheered someone up) When you cheer someone up, you make them stop feeling sad and they become happier.

chill /tʃɪl/ – (chills, chilling, chilled) To chill something means to make it cold.

claw /klɔ/ – (claws) The claws of a bird or animal are the thin, hard, curved nails at the end of its feet.

clerk /klɜrk/ – (clerks) A clerk is a person who works in an office, bank, or law court and whose job is to keep the records or accounts and deal with customers.

coal miners /koʊl maɪnər/ – Coal miners are people who dig deep holes or tunnels in the ground in order to obtain coal, which is a hard, black substance that is burned as fuel.

coldhearted /koʊldhɑrtɪd/ – Someone who is coldhearted is marked by a lack of sympathy, interest, or sensitivity.

complain /kəmpleɪn/ – (complains, complaining, complained) If you're complaining about something, you're saying that you are not satisfied with it.

contagious /kənteɪdʒəs/ – A contagious disease can be caught by touching people or things that are infected with it.

countinghouse /kaʊntɪŋ haʊs/ – (countinghouses) A countinghouse is a building, room, or office used for keeping books and transacting business.

crutch /krʌtʃ/ – (crutches) A crutch is a stick which someone with an injured foot or leg uses to support them when walking.

D

dead as a doornail /dɛd əz ə dɔrneɪl/ – If you say that someone is dead as doornail, you're saying that you know for a fact that that person is dead and has been dead for a long time.

deathbed /dɛθbɛd/ – (deathbeds) A deathbed is the bed in which a person dies. You can say someone is on their deathbed if they are at their last hours of life.

debt /dɛt/ – (debts) A debt is a sum of money that you owe someone.

deserve /dɪzɜrv/ – (deserves, deserving, deserved) If you say that a person or thing deserves something, you mean that they should have it or receive it because of their actions or qualities.

dismay /dɪsmeɪ/ – (dismays, dismaying, dismayed) Dismay is a strong feeling of fear, worry, or sadness that is caused by something unpleasant and unexpected.

donate /doʊneɪt/ – (donates, donating, donated) If you donate something to charity or other organization, you give it to them.

door knocker /dɔr nɒkər/ – (door knockers) A door knocker is a metal ring, bar, or hammer hinged to the front of a door that you use to make a tapping noise so people on the other side know you're there.

E

embarrass /ɪmbærəs/ – (embarrasses, embarrassing, embarrassed) If something or someone embarrasses you, they make you feel shy or ashamed.

enjoyable /ɪndʒɔɪəbəl/ – Something that is enjoyable gives you pleasure.

F

feast /fist/ – (feasts) A feast is a large and special meal.

funeral /fyunərəl/ – (funerals) A funeral is the ceremony that is held when the body of someone who has died is buried or cremated.

G

game /geɪm/ – (games) A game is an activity or sport, usually involving skill, knowledge, or chance, in which you follow fixed rules and try to win against an opponent.

gather /gæðər/ – (gathers, gathering, gathered) If people gather somewhere, or if someone gathers them, they come together in a group.

generous /dʒɛnərəs/ – (generously) A generous person gives more of something, especially money, than is usual or expected.

ghost /goust/ – (ghosts) A ghost is the spirit of a dead person that someone believes they can see or feel.

grow /grouɪŋ/ – (grows, growing, grown) You use grow to say that someone or something gradually changes until they have a new quality, feeling, or attitude.

guide /gaɪd/ – (guides, guiding, guided) If you guide someone somewhere, you go there with them in order to show them the way.

H

headstone /hɛdstoun/ – (headstones) A headstone is a memorial stone at the head of a grave.

hearse /hɜrs/ – (hearses) A hearse is the name for any vehicle used to transport the dead to the grave.

huge /hyudʒ/ – Something or someone that is huge is extremely large in size, amount, or degree.

humbug /hʌmbʌg/ – You would say something is humbug if you think it is something designed to deceive or mislead.

I

ignorance /ɪgnərəns/ – Someone who demonstrates ignorance does not know things that they should know. If someone is ignorant of a fact, they do not know it.

in one's name /ɪn wʌnz neɪm/ – If you do something in the name of an ideal or an abstract thing, you do it in order to preserve or promote that thing.

J

journey /dʒɜrni/ – (journeys) When you make a journey, you travel from one place to another.

K

keep an eye on /kip ən aɪ ɒn/ – (keeps an eye on, keeping an eye on, kept an eye on) If you keep your eye on someone or something, you watch them carefully.

L

lame /leɪm/ – If someone is lame, they are unable to walk properly because of damage to one or both of their legs.

lesson /lɛsᵊn/ – (lessons) You use lesson to refer to an experience which acts as a warning to you or an example from which you should learn.

link /lɪŋk/ – (links) A link is one of the rings in a chain.

M

make up for /meɪk ʌp fɔr/ – If you try to make up for something, you try to compensate for a deficiency or omission you previously had or made.

master /mæstər/ – (masters) A master is the male head of a household or a boy too young to be called mister.

measure /mɛʒər/ – (measures, measuring, measured) If you measure the quality, quantity, or value of something, you find out or judge how great it is.

mercy /mɜrsi/ – If someone in authority shows mercy, they choose not to harm or punish someone they have power over.

merry /mɛri/ – Merry means happy and cheerful.

meet one's maker /mit wʌnz meɪkər/ – If you say that someone has met his maker, you are saying that this person has died.

miser /maɪzər/ – (misers) A miser is a mean person, especially one who is extremely stingy with money.

N

nephew /nɛfyu/ – (nephews) Someone's nephew is the son of their sister or brother.

nightmare /naɪtmɛər/ – (nightmares)
A nightmare is a very frightening dream.

O

observe /əbzɛrv/ – (observes, observing, observed) If you observe something such as a law or custom, you obey it or follow it.

P

parliament /pɑrləmənt/ – (parliaments) The parliament of some countries is the group of people who make or change its laws.

parlor /pɑrlər/ – (parlors) A room used primarily for conversation or the reception of guests.

partner /pɑrtnər/ – (partners) The partners in a firm or business are the people who share the ownership of it.

partridge /pɑrtʃrɪdʒ/ – (partridges) A partridge is a medium-sized and stout-bodied bird that is often hunted for food or sport.

patience /peɪtʃᵊns/ – If you have patience, you are able to stay calm and not get annoyed, for example, when something takes a long time.

Poor Law /puər lɔ/ – The Poor Law is a law providing for or regulating the public relief or support of the poor.

pounds /paʊndz/ – Pounds are the units of money which are used in Britain. They are represented by the symbol £. Some other countries, such as Egypt, also have units of money called pounds.

praise /preɪz/ – (praises) If you praise someone or something, you express approval for their achievements or qualities.

prison /prɪzᵊn/ – (prisons) A prison is a building where criminals are kept as punishment.

provide /prəvaɪd/ – (provides, providing, provided) If you provide for someone, you support them financially and make sure that they have the things that they need.

punishes oneself /pʌnɪʃɪz wʌnsɛlf/ – If you punish yourself, you are making yourself

suffer in some way because you think you have done something wrong.

R

raise /reɪz/ – (raises) A raise is an increase in your wages or salary.

raise money /reɪz mʌni/ – (raises money, raising money, raised money) If you raise money for a charity or an institution, you ask people for money that you collect on its behalf.

recognize /rɛkəgnaɪz/ – (recognizes, recognizing, recognized) If you recognize someone or something, you know who that person is or what that thing is because you have seen or heard them before.

regret /rɪgrɛt/ – (regrets) Regret is a feeling of sadness or disappointment, which is caused by something that has happened or something that you have done or not done.

relationship /rɪlaɪʃᵊnʃɪp/ – (relationships) A relationship is a close friendship between two people, especially one involving romantic feelings.

remove /rimuv/ – (removes, removing, removed) If you remove something from a place, you take it away.

reveal /rɪvil/ – (reveals, revealing, revealed) If you reveal something that has been out of sight, you uncover it so that people can see it.

robe /roʊb/ – (robes) A robe is a loose piece of clothing, usually worn in official or religious ceremonies.

S

sea /si/ – (seas) The sea is the salty water that covers about three-quarters of the Earth's surface.

seat /sit/ – (seats) A seat is an object that you can sit on, such as a chair.

servant /sɜrvᵊnt/ – (servants) Servants are people who are employed to work at another person's home, such as a cleaner or gardener.

show off /ʃoʊ ɔf/ – (shows off, showing off, showed off) If you show off a talent, object, or skill, you perform or display it proudly for people to see.

skill /skɪl/ – (skills) A skill is a type of work or activity which requires special training and knowledge.

soften /sɔfᵊn/ – (softens, softening, softened) If something has softened, it has become less hard, stiff, or firm. If a person softens, they become more sympathetic and less hostile or critical.

spread /sprɛd/ – (spreads, spreading) If you spread something somewhere, you open it out or arrange it over a place or surface so that all of it can be seen or used easily. If a feeling or idea spreads or is spread by people, it gradually reaches or affects a larger and larger area or more and more people.

squeeze /skwiz/ – (squeezes, squeezing, squeezed) To squeeze something means to fit it into a small space.

stingy /stɪndʒi/ – If someone is stingy, they are not generous and usually give, spend, or use very little.

struggling /strʌgᵊlɪŋ/ – If someone or something is struggling, they are making strong efforts in the face of difficulties or opposition.

suffer /sʌfər/ – (suffers, suffering, suffered) If you suffer, you are badly affected by an event or situation.

T

take care of /teɪk kɛər əf / – If you take care of someone or something, you look

after them and prevent them from being harmed or damaged.

toast /toʊst/ – (toasts, toasting, toasted) If you toast someone, you drink some wine or other alcoholic drink in order to show your appreciation of them or to wish them success.

toothpick /tuθpɪk/ – (toothpicks) A toothpick is a pointed instrument that is used to remove bits of food stuck between your teeth.

travel /trævᵊl/ – (travels, traveling, traveled) If you travel, you go from one place to another, often to a place that is far away.

tremble /trɛmbᵊl/ – (trembles, trembling, trembled) If something trembles, it shakes slightly.

trivial /trɪviəl/ – If you describe something as trivial, you think that it is unimportant and not serious.

W

wandering /wɒndərɪŋ/ – If you are wandering someplace, you are walking around there in a casual way, often without the intent to go in any particular direction.

want /wɒnt/ – Want is grave or extreme poverty that deprives one of the necessities of life.

wellbeing /wɛlbiɪŋ/ – Someone's wellbeing is their health and happiness.

workhouse /wɜrkhaʊs/ – (workhouses) A workhouse is another word for a poor house, which is a place maintained at public expense to shelter needy or dependent people.

Charles Dickens's Life

Charles Dickens was born on February 7, 1812. He lived near the sea in southeast England until he was nine years old. He was the second of eight children born to John and Elizabeth Dickens. Dickens's father, John, was a kind and likable man. However, he was not very good with money and made many debts throughout his life. The Dickens family were comfortable for a while and sent Dickens to a fee-paying school when he was nine. By the time he was ten, however, they moved to London, and when he was 12, his father was arrested and taken to debtors' prison.

Dickens's mother and his seven brothers and sisters moved into prison with their father, which was common at the time. Mrs. Dickens arranged for young Charles to live alone outside the prison and work with other children. He pasted labels on bottles in a blacking warehouse (blacking was a type of manufactured soot used to make black pigment for products such as matches). Dickens found the three months he spent apart from his family very distressing. Not only did he hate the job, but he considered himself too good for it. He never forgot this terrible experience. His great grandmother died and left enough money to pay off the debts and get his father released from prison.

Once his father was allowed out of prison, Dickens returned to school. He eventually became a law clerk, and then a court reporter. From 1830 to 1836, Dickens wrote for a number of newspapers as a journalist. In 1833, his first published story, "A Dinner at Poplar Walk," was published. Soon after, he began to write his series for *The Chronicle*.

On April 2, 1836, Charles Dickens married Catherine Hogarth (the daughter of his editor, George Hogarth). They had ten children (seven boys and three girls). Also in 1836, Dickens published the first series of *Sketches by Boz*. (Boz was a pen name used by Dickens).

After this, Dickens finally became a full-time novelist. His first novel, *The Pickwick Papers*, became a huge success when Dickens was only 25. He wrote novels very quickly, writing *Oliver Twist* as a monthly series between 1837 and 1839. In 1843, his dearly loved Christmas tale, *A Christmas Carol*, was published. It sold 5,000 copies on Christmas Eve — and has never been out of print since.

Unfortunately, Dickens's personal life was not as successful. He separated from his wife, Catherine, in 1858 and denied having an affair. Although his work promoted family values, Dickens appeared to have been having an affair with an actress called Ellen Lawless Ternan. He tried very hard to keep his personal life private.

However, Dickens continued to publish extensively. He became well-known internationally, traveling to Canada and the United States twice, as well as to Europe. He gave many public readings of his works, even after his doctors advised him to rest.

Dickens didn't listen; he began work on one last novel, *The Mystery of Edwin Drood*. This work was never finished. Dickens suffered a stroke and died suddenly on June 9, 1870. Although Charles Dickens asked to be buried in a simple and private manner, he was so popular that the public insisted for him to be recognized as a great writer.

He was buried at Westminster Abbey. His funeral, however, was private, with only 12 people present. After the service, thousands of people came to pay their respects. Today, a small stone marks his grave and simply says: "Charles Dickens Born 7th February 1812 Died 9th June 1870

Dickens Timeline

1812

February 7: Charles John Huffam Dickens is born in Landport, Portsmouth, England.

1817

April: The Dickens family moves to Chatham, Kent.

1821

March: Dickens goes to school next door to the family home.

1822

September: The Dickens family moves to Camden Town, London.

1824

February: Dickens (age 12) goes to work at Warren's Blacking Factory. His father is arrested for debt and sent with his family to Marshalsea Prison.

May: The Dickens family is released from prison.

June: Dickens leaves the Blacking Factory and is enrolled in Wellington House Academy.

1827

May: Dickens becomes a law clerk at Lincoln's Inn and studies shorthand.

1828

November: Dickens becomes a freelance reporter at Doctors' Commons Court.

1830

Dickens becomes a parliamentary reporter for the *True Sun* newspaper.

1832

March: Dickens begins work for the *Mirror of Parliament* newspaper.

1833

December: Dickens publishes his first story, "A Dinner at Poplar Walk," in *The Old Monthly Magazine.*

1834

August: Dickens begins working at the *Morning Chronicle* newspaper and writes articles under the name "Boz."

November: Dickens's father is arrested for debt again. Dickens helps him.

1836

February: Dickens's first series of articles, *Sketches by Boz,* is published.

March: The first part of *Pickwick Papers* appears in its serialized form and runs for a year.

April: Dickens marries Catherine Hogarth, daughter of George Hogarth, the editor of the *Evening Chronicle.*

December: Dickens becomes the editor of *Bentley's Miscellany* and publishes his second series of articles called *Sketches by Boz.*

1837

February: Dickens begins writing *Oliver Twist.* It appears monthly in *Bentley's Miscellany* until 1839.

May: Catherine's younger sister Mary, whom Dickens idolizes, dies.

1838

March: Dickens's *Nicholas Nickelby* is serialized. It runs until 1839.

1839

January: Dickens resigns as editor of *Bentley's Miscellany.*

1840

April: Dickens begins the serialization of *The Old Curiosity Shop.* It runs for a year in *Master Humphrey's Clock.*

1842

January: Dickens travels to Canada and United States.

June: Dickens returns to London and declines the offer to run for Parliament

October: Dickens begins writing *American Notes.*

1843

January: Serialization of *Martin Chuzzlewit* begins.

December: Dickens publishes *A Christmas Carol,* the first of his Christmas books.

1845

September: Dickens's amateur theater company gives its first performance, "Every Man in his Humour."

1846

July: Dickens begins writing *Dombey and Son,* which runs until April 1848.

1848

December: Dickens publishes his final Christmas book, *The Haunted Man.*

1849

May: *David Copperfield* is serialized monthly until November 1850.

1851

March: Dickens's father dies.

April: Dickens's infant daughter, Dora, dies.

1852

March: *Bleak House* first appears.

1853

December: Dickens gives his first public reading of *A Christmas Carol* in Birmingham. He gives the reading to raise money for charity.

1854

April–August: *Hard Times* appears weekly in *Household Words*.

1855

December: *Little Dorrit* appears monthly until 1857.

1856

March: Dickens purchases Gads Hill in Rochester, Kent.

1857

July: Dickens performs for Queen Victoria.

August: Dickens meets and falls in love with a young actress named Ellen Lawless Ternan.

1858

April: Dickens begins a series of public readings (for profit) in London and continues his provincial tour.

May: Dickens separates from his wife, Catherine. Her sister, Georgina, looks after the household.

1860

September: Dickens intentionally burns many of his personal letters.

December: Dickens begins writing *Great Expectations*.

1863

September: Dickens's mother, Elizabeth Dickens, dies.

December: Dickens's son, Walter, dies in India.

1864

February: Dickens's health worsens, probably due to overwork.

May: *Our Mutual Friend* runs monthly until 1865.

1865

June: Dickens is badly shaken after being involved in the Staplehurst Railway Accident while traveling back from France with Ellen Lawless Ternan and her mother.

1867

November: Against his doctors' advice, Dickens continues public readings in England and Ireland and goes on an American reading tour.

1868

April: Dickens returns to England and continues his series of readings.

1869

Dickens suffers a mild stroke. He cancels his provincial readings.

September: Dickens begins to write *The Mystery of Edwin Drood* and draws up his will.

1870

March: Dickens has a private audience with Queen Victoria. His final public readings take place in London.

June 9: Dickens dies at Gads Hill after suffering a stroke. He is buried on June 14 at Westminster Abbey.

September: *The Mystery of Edwin Drood* appears (posthumously).

Hard Times

The Victorian era (1837–1901) represented the height of the Industrial Revolution. It was a period of major social, economic, and technological change in Great Britain. Queen Victoria's reign also saw an expansion of the British Empire. Britain became the most important global power at that time.

It was a time of inventors and inventions and of rapid progress in science, technology, and medicine. From the steam engine to the steam printer, from the skyscraper to the machine gun, from the flush toilet to photography, moving pictures, electricity, the telegraph, and telephone, the Victorian era was a transition from the old, traditional world to the new, modern age.

Railroads revolutionized travel as a method of transporting goods and people. Although the first rail connection (from Stockton to Darlington) opened years before Victoria became queen, the early years of her reign witnessed the so-called "railway fever." In 1850, there were 6,000 miles of track in Britain. By 1901, there were almost 35,000 miles of track. Railroads changed the way people lived and worked.

Many important, new developments, such as the postal service (the "Penny Post"), could not have happened without the railroads. As technology

Queen Victoria

allowed people to travel farther and faster, the world was divided into 24 time zones. Greenwich, England became the center of the world's time.

But this new Britain was not a paradise for everyone. With this rapid progress came changes in terms of population size, jobs, and the way people lived. The population in Great Britain trippled between 1800 and 1900. People flocked to the cities to work in the new factories. Housing became overcrowded and unsanitary. London was the area most affected. New technology generated a lot of wealth for the rich. The underpaid workforce consisted of adults and children living in poverty. Millions of workers lived in slums or in unfit housing. They had no sanitation, no fresh water, no paved streets, no schools, no law and order, no decent food, and little fuel for cooking or heating.

Children had to help their families by earning wages like the adults, as Dickens himself did in Warren's Blacking Factory. They often worked long hours in dangerous conditions for a few pennies a day.

There were also many homeless children. They survived by begging and stealing. To the respectable Victorians, the homeless children must have seemed a real threat to society. Something had to be done about them to preserve law and order.

Many people believed that education was the answer. A number of "ragged schools" were started to help meet that need. These were schools that were funded by donations. They provided poor children a free education. They often provided food, clothing, and a place to live in addition to basic education. Dickens visited Field Lane Ragged School in 1843. This made a lasting impression on him. It was a major influence when he wrote *A Christmas Carol*.

In 1870, an act of parliament allowed "board schools" to be paid for with local funds. This allowed more children to attend school. But it took another 11 years before children were required to attend school until the age of 10. And it took 9 more years before free, public education was available to all children.

The government also began to pass laws that protected children in the workplace. The first Factory Act (1819) prohibited children under the age of 9 from working in factories and children aged 9 to 16 from working more than 72 hours per week.

In 1833, a another law limited the working hours for children 9 to 13 years old. They could work no more than 48 hours per week in textile factories. The Mines Act of 1842 stopped women and boys under 10 from working in mines. Additional Factory Acts in 1844 and 1847 established the 12-hour workday for women and the 6 1/2-hour workday for children under 13. These laws were enforced by factory inspectors. But the inspectors were often so poorly paid that they were easily bribed. Many parents were often so desperate for money that they lied about the ages of their children so the children could work. Before 1837, births did not have to be registered. Without a birth certificate, it was impossible for anyone to prove the age of a child.

Life was very harsh. In addition to appalling working conditions, low wages, slum housing, and disease, the majority of the population had no way to change their circumstances. Nowhere was this more clearly seen than in the writings of Charles Dickens.

A Very Victorian Christmas

Before Christianity arrived in northern Europe, people celebrated a 12-day midwinter "Yule" festival. This is the origin of the decorating with evergreen plants, such as mistletoe, holly, and ivy, and burning the yule log at Christmas. When the Julian calendar was introduced, this festival was set on December 25 and was combined with Christian celebrations to create what we now call Christmas.

Reinventing Christmas

The Victorian era saw the reinvention of Christmas in Britain. When Queen Victoria's reign began in 1837, few people celebrated Christmas. No one had heard of Santa Claus, Christmas cards had not been invented, most people were not allowed time off from work, and few people had extra money to buy gifts or extra food. But this all began to change.

The wealth generated by the new factories and industries gave middle-class families the opportunity to take time off and celebrate the holiday season on Christmas Day (December 25) and Boxing Day (December 26). The development of the railroads also allowed the people who had moved to the towns and cities in search of work to return home for Christmas with their families.

Children's toys that used to be handmade and expensive were more affordable because of mass production in factories.

However, they were still too expensive for working families and the poor whose Christmas stockings (which first became popular around 1870) would contain only an apple, an orange, and a few nuts or maybe a small, homemade gift.

Food was a major part of the festivities. In northern England, roast beef was the traditional Christmas dinner; in London and the south, the tradition was to serve goose. Many of the poor had to eat rabbit. Not until the end of the century did most people eat turkey for their Christmas dinner.

The introduction of a national postal service in 1840 allowed people to send Christmas cards. The first Christmas card was created in 1843 by Sir Henry Cole, a wealthy British businessman who wanted a card to send his friends and professional acquaintances to wish them a "Merry Christmas."

A Royal Celebration

Queen Victoria loved to celebrate Christmas. She described it as a "most dear happy time." She had 9 children, so her Christmases became large family occasions. Many of the royal Christmas traditions were described in her personal diaries and in the newspapers of the day. These traditions included decorated trees, sending cards, a lavish family meal, and giving gifts to the poor. It was Queen Charlotte (Queen Victoria's grandmother and wife of George III) who brought the German tradition of Christmas trees to England. They were a feature of Victoria's Christmas festivities from childhood.

In her journal for Christmas Eve 1832, the 13-year-old Princess

Victoria wrote:

> After dinner ... we then went into the drawing-room near the dining-room. ... There were two large round tables on which were placed two trees hung with lights and sugar ornaments. All the presents being placed [a]round the trees ...

And for those less fortunate?

The Victorian era was one of stark contrasts, and Christmas was no exception. For the very poor, the Christmas season made little difference in their lives.

Following the example set by Queen Victoria, it became fashionable for the middle class to give alms (gifts of money, clothing, or food) to the poor. (This is what the businessmen are trying to organize with Scrooge on page 17). The custom of giving gifts and food to the poor on Boxing Day (December 26) was also revived in this period. Churches opened their alms boxes and distributed money to the poor.

For people without jobs or homes of their own, the workhouse provided the venue for Christmas celebrations. Before

1834, Christmas Day meant a treat for most of the residents of the parish workhouse. However, with the advent of union workhouses set up by the 1834 Poor Law Amendment Act, no extra food was given on Christmas Day (or any other feast day). Despite that Christmas Day was a special day when the workhouse residents rested. It took 6 years for the rules to be revised to allow extra treats — but only if they came from private sources and not from union funds. A change in the ruling in 1847 finally allowed for Christmas extras from the workhouse funds.

With the exception of the very poor, Victorian Christmases were a time of celebration and of families gathering together with the prospect of a feast (however small) and entertainment — all o which is captured in the most famous "Christmas book" of all time — *A Christmas Carol*.

A Christmas Carol

The idea for Dickens's first "Christmas book," the best-lov

nd most read of all of his ooks, came from his travels round England, where he saw hildren working in horrible onditions. Dickens believed that ducation was a remedy for rime and poverty. This belief, ong with scenes he had itnessed at the Field Lane agged School, made Dickens solve to "strike a sledge ammer blow" for the poor.

As the idea for the story took shape and he began writing, Dickens became engrossed in the book. He later wrote that as the tale unfolded, he "wept and laughed, and wept again" and that

> thinking whereof he walked about the black streets of London fifteen or twenty miles many a night when all of the sober folks had gone to bed.

A Christmas Carol took just six weeks to complete. It was published on December 17, 1843. It was an overwhelming success. It sold more than 5,000 copies by Christmas Eve.

It is a book of enduring appeal. For many people, it has become part of the festival of Christmas itself and is one of the best-loved Christmas stories in the world.

Character Summary

Ebenezer Scrooge

Scrooge is the main character. At the beginning of the story, he is a cold and selfish man. He is very rich and does not want to share his money with anybody. He does not like poor people and does nothing to help them. He was a poor and lonely boy. As he grew older, he looked toward money as a way to gain power and control. The visits from the ghosts help Scrooge to see how he should change.

Ghost of Jacob Marley

Marley worked with Scrooge when he was alive. He had a similar personality to Scrooge and was not kind to others. Marley's ghost visits Scrooge to warn him of what will happen if Scrooge continues to be selfish and uncaring. Marley's ghost tells Scrooge that he still has a chance to change his ways and that three ghosts will visit Scrooge.

Ghost of Christmas Past

The Ghost of Christmas Past glows and uses a cap to hide the light shining from its head. This ghost shows Scrooge Christmases from his past. Scrooge sees himself as a lonely boy, a happy apprentice, and a selfish young man. The scenes from his past upset Scrooge a lot.

Ghost of Christmas Present

The Ghost of Christmas Present is a huge giant who wears a green robe. His life is as long as Christmas Day. He shows Scrooge how people will celebrate Christmas the very next day. The ghost shows Scrooge the Cratchit family Christmas, and Scrooge sees that Tiny Tim will not survive if his life doesn't change. The ghost also shows Scrooge coal miners, sailors on a ship at sea, and his nephew, Fred, all happily celebrating Christmas. As they travel, the ghost sprinkles Christmas happiness on people and they enjoy Christmas even more. The ghost explains to Scrooge that Christmas happiness helps poor people the most because they need the most help.

Ghost of Christmas to Come

The Ghost of Christmas to Come is dressed in a dark robe and does not speak. He shows Scrooge what Christmas in the future will look like if Scrooge doesn't change his ways. The ghost shows Scrooge that he will die all alone and that nobody will be sad over his death. This scares Scrooge very much.

Character Summary

Fred

Fred is Scrooge's nephew, the daughter of Scrooge's sister Fan. He is a kind man who always invites Scrooge to eat Christmas dinner with him. He promises to always invite Scrooge over until the day he dies.

Bob Cratchit

Bob Cratchit works as a clerk at Scrooge's countinghouse. He is a cheerful man who loves Christmas. He is very poor and has a large family. Scrooge makes Bob work long hours and does not pay him enough.

Mrs. Cratchit

Mrs. Cratchit is Bob's wife. She is a kind and loving woman, but she does not like Scrooge.

Tiny Tim Cratchit

Tiny Tim is Bob and Mrs. Cratchit's son. He cannot walk and uses a crutch. Even though his family is poor and he is very sick, he is a happy little boy. And his family loves him very much.

Important Quotations

Location	Dickens's Original	Adapted Text
Chapter One Page 9	External heat and cold had little influence on Scrooge. No warmth could warm, no wintry weather chill him. No wind that blew was bitterer than he, no falling snow was more intent upon its purpose, no pelting rain less open to entreaty.	Heat couldn't warm him, and cold couldn't chill him.
Chapter One Page 13	"If I could work my will," said Scrooge indignantly, "every idiot who goes about with 'Merry Christmas' on his lips, should be boiled with his own pudding, and buried with a stake of holly through his heart. He should!"	"If I had my way, every idiot who says 'Merry Christmas' would be cooked in his own Christmas meal!"
Chapter One Page 14	"But I am sure I have always thought of Christmas time, when it has come round — apart from the veneration due to its sacred name and origin, if anything belonging to it can be apart from that — as a good time; a kind, forgiving, charitable, pleasant time: the only time I know of, in the long calendar of the year, when men and women seem by one consent to open their shut-up hearts freely, and to think of people below them as if they really were fellow-passengers to the grave, and not another race of creatures bound on other journeys. And therefore, uncle, though it has never put a scrap of gold or silver in my pocket, I believe that it has done me good, and will do me good; and I say, God bless it!'"	"Things don't have to make money to be good, Uncle. Christmas is a good time— a time when men and women are friendlier and kinder. So, it has been good for me. And it will continue to be good for me. And I say, God bless it!"
Chapter One Page 30	"You may be an undigested bit of beef, a blot of mustard, a crumb of cheese, a fragment of underdone potato. There's more of gravy than of grave about you, whatever you are!"	"I can't trust my eyes. Maybe something I ate has made me sick."
Chapter Three Page 76	"There are some upon this earth of yours," returned the Spirit, "who lay claim to know us, and who do their deeds of passion, pride, ill-will, hatred, envy, bigotry, and selfishness in our name, who are as strange to us and all out kith and kin, as if they had never lived. Remember that, and charge their doings on themselves, not us."	"Some people on Earth do bad things in our name. Remember that. And don't blame us!"
Chapter Four Page 123	"Men's courses will foreshadow certain ends, to which, if persevered in, they must lead," said Scrooge. "But if the courses be departed from, the ends will change. Say it is thus with what you show me!"	"If we change how we act, then we change our lives, too. Please tell me that this applies to what you have shown me!"
Chapter Five Pages 139–140	Scrooge was better than his word. He did it all, and infinitely more; and to Tiny Tim, who did not die, he was a second father. He became as good a friend, as good a master, and as good a man, as the good old city knew, or any other good old city, town, or borough, in the good old world. Some people laughed to see the alteration in him, but he let them laugh, and little heeded them; for he was wise enough to know that nothing ever happened on this globe, for good, at which some people did not have their fill of laughter in the outset; and knowing that such as these would be blind anyway, he thought it quite as well that they should wrinkle up their eyes in grins, as have the malady in less attractive forms. His own heart laughed: and that was quite enough for him.	Scrooge did even more than he said he would do. Tiny Tim did not die. Scrooge was like his second father. Scrooge became a good man. Some people laughed when they saw how he had changed. But Scrooge didn't care. He was happy just to see them laughing. He was happy in his heart. And that was good enough for him.

Notes

OTHER CLASSICAL COMICS TITLES:
Henry V   1-4240-2877-9

Frankenstein   1-4240-3184-2

Great Expectations   1-4240-2882-5

Macbeth   1-4240-2873-6

Jane Eyre   1-4240-2887-6

Romeo and Juliet   1-4240-4291-7

COMING SOON:
The Tempest   1-4240-4296-8